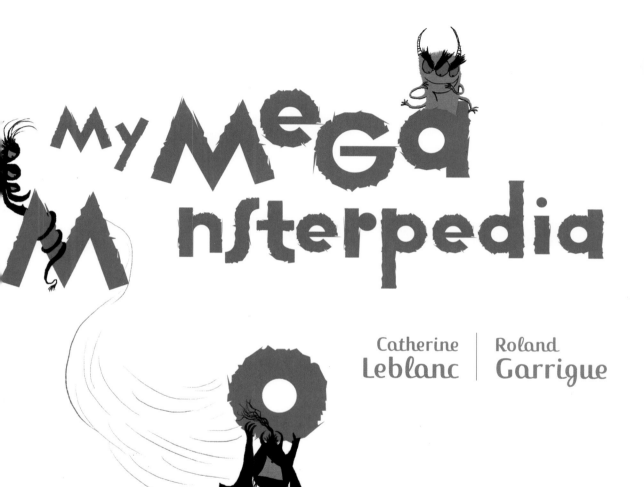

My MeGa Mⁿsterpedia

Catherine **Leblanc** | Roland **Garrigue**

INSIGHT KIDS

San Rafael, California

Monsters

of all shapes and sizes sometimes try to scare us.

What better way to identify and get rid of them
than an encyclopedia of monsters?

Some monsters are nice and just a **little** annoying	but others are **mean**	and some are **very mean!**

(1) Monsters can live on land, in water, or in the air. (2) They can come out during the day or night. They can be tiny or huge. (3) They can change shape and color.
They can make strange noises, smell nice, or really stink.

Either way, the more you know about them, the less frightened you'll be.

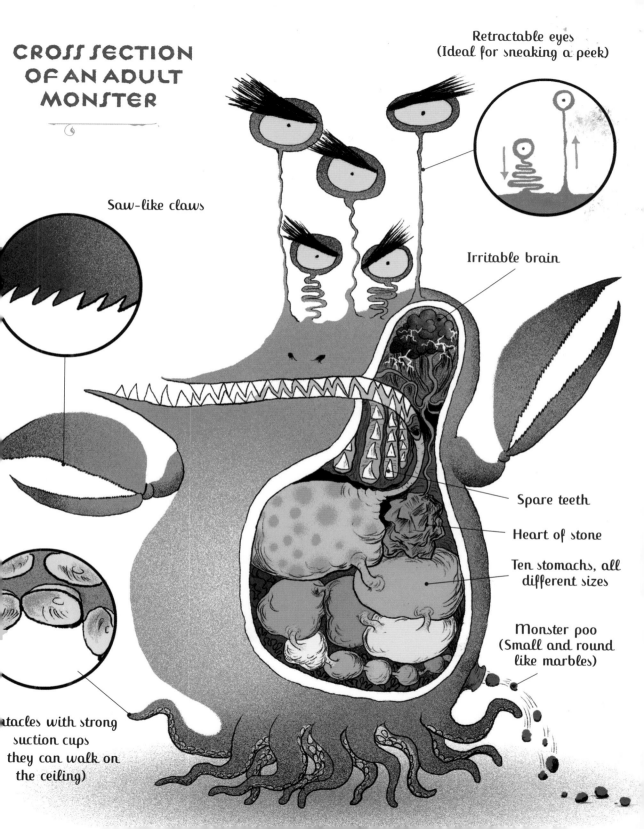

CROSS SECTION OF AN ADULT MONSTER

Retractable eyes
(Ideal for sneaking a peek)

Saw-like claws

Irritable brain

Spare teeth

Heart of stone

Ten stomachs, all
different sizes

Monster poo
(Small and round
like marbles)

...tacles with strong
suction cups
...they can walk on
the ceiling)

Alphabeast

This little monster scrambles up all the letters of the alphabet and makes it impossible to find any words alphabetically!

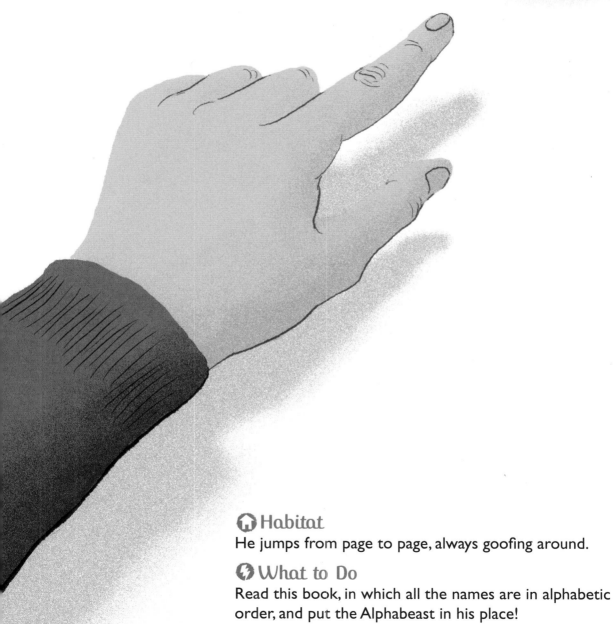

🏠 Habitat
He jumps from page to page, always goofing around.

⚡ What to Do
Read this book, in which all the names are in alphabetic order, and put the Alphabeast in his place!

Aysnortuptoys

This one sucks up all the toys lying peacefully on the rug.

🏠 Habitat

He lives in closets, and since he can only come out when there are toys lying around, he mostly moans and complains about being trapped for long periods of time.

⚡ What to Do

Clean up all your toys, except for a game of pick-up-sticks; it'll give him a terrible stomachache.

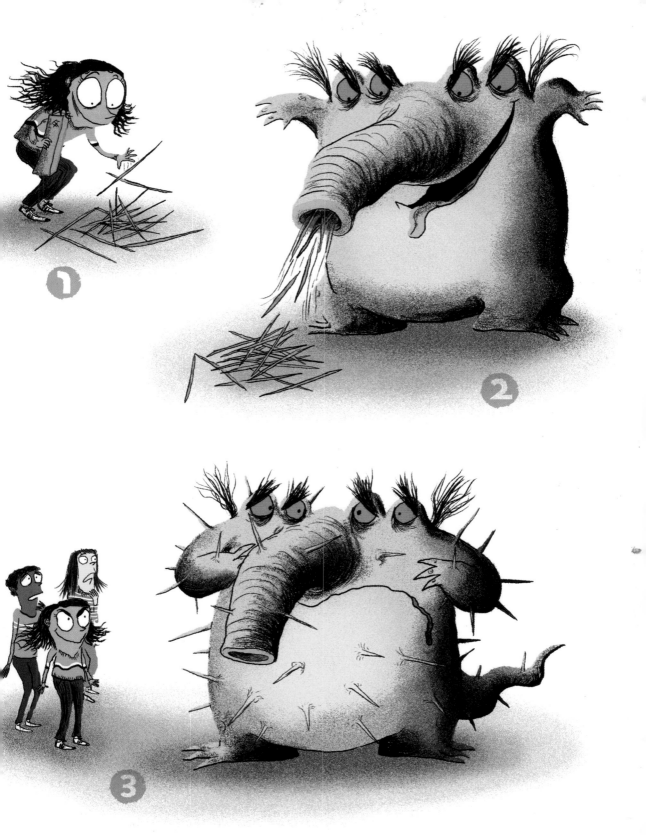

Botherinbobby

When you're trying to get work done, this monster walks all over your desk to distract you.

🏠 Habitat
You can sometimes find him at home, but he prefers the classroom.

〰 Weakness
Wimpy and skittish

⚡ What to Do
Whistle—it'll frighten him away.

Brutus Spitballus

She hates to see you concentrate. Whenever you're trying to write something, she bounces off your head.

🏠 Habitat
Her favorite place is the classroom, where she has a tendency to multiply.

⚫ Weakness
Is easily flustered

⚡ What to Do (But it's risky!)
Redirect her toward the trash can, but avoid the teacher at all costs.

Cravels

These tough little creatures get into your shoes
and crunch on your feet.

⌂ Habitat
You can sometimes find them in your sneakers, but they prefer sandals.

⚡ What to Do
Give your shoes a good shake.

Creepinpoop

He lies in wait, cackling, then throws himself under your shoe.

⬆ Habitat
Sidewalks

⊘ Weakness
He's no genius and is easily crushed
beneath your foot!

⚡ What to Do
Get rid of what's left!

Danitemare

Grabs hold of you when you're asleep and drags you into a nightmare. We're all really quite sick of this trick.

Habitat
The dark of night

What to Do
When you're awake, he cannot stay. Open your eyes and poof! He'll go away. Then have good dreams all night you may.

Drainbane

A very scary one. He lives in the toilet and tries to drag you into the sewer.

⚙ Survival Strategy
Flush! And he'll be the one to disappear.

◉ He has one way of getting back at you:
He eats toilet paper, so when you reach for it, he makes sure that there's none left. . . .

Embarrassassino

A big cuddly creature who isn't mean but doesn't know when to stop. She suffocates you with hugs and kisses.

Habitat
Feels at home with family and friends

What to Do
To ward her off, put mustard on your cheek.

Fogdibrain

He scrambles numbers in your head so that you make mistakes.

⌂ Habitat
Math homework

⚡ What to Do
Crumple up the page, and you will mash him up at the same time. Then start with a new page with fresh ideas.

Frreezinkold

An ice monster that gives you the chills
and tries to freeze you solid.

🏠 Habitat
He lives outside and shows up mostly in winter. He hibernates during the summer.

⚙ Survival Strategy
Run! That will warm you up and melt him at the same time.

Fynderzkeeperz

He searches through your things, borrows whateve
he wants, and hardly ever returns anything.

🏠 Habitat
In your home, as often as possible

⚡ What to Do
Look for him in his favorite hiding places: the trash can, a toy chest,
a pile of socks, or your brother's room . . .

Gickiegoober

A yucky bit in the middle of your plate of food.
The cafeteria lady is hoping that you'll eat it!

⌂ Habitat
Some school cafeterias

⚡ What to Do (Note: Not highly recommended)
Eat everything around it so it can't get to the rest of your food.
Once you're done, make sure to throw it away.

He's what makes you fidget. He itches even more when you scratch.

He's happiest under your clothes.

Take a shower—a long one is best.

Hallucinator

He hides in the dark and projects all kinds of shadows—
the scarier the better.

🏠 Habitat
In dark corners, at the ends
of hallways, and in caves.

⚡ What to Do
He loses his powers as soon
as the light is turned on. His
show is over, and his tricks
no longer fool anyone.

Horrorkane

He makes terrible angry noises! Rumbling. Thunder.
It can be horrifying!

🏠 Habitat
This black beast comes down from the sky.

⚡ What to Do
Stay inside. Let him wear himself out.
You're safe indoors!

Icky Yicky

This monster is pretty disgusting. It's best to avoid him.

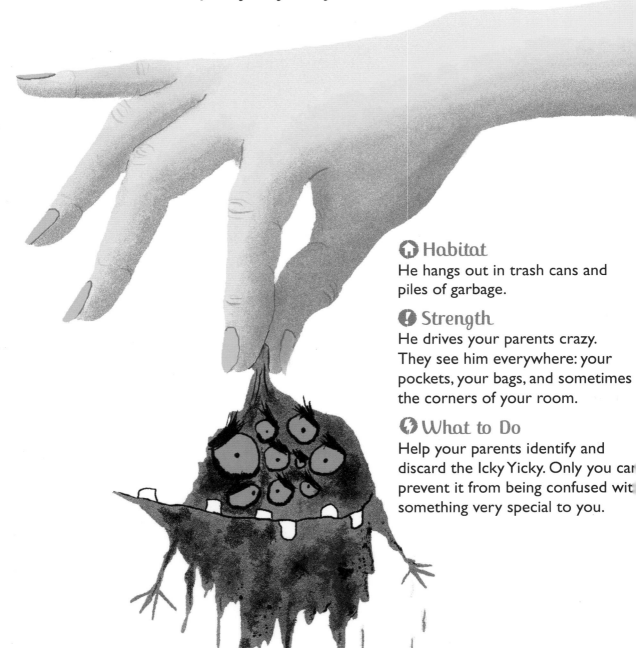

⬆ Habitat

He hangs out in trash cans and piles of garbage.

⚡ Strength

He drives your parents crazy. They see him everywhere: your pockets, your bags, and sometimes the corners of your room.

⚡ What to Do

Help your parents identify and discard the Icky Yicky. Only you can prevent it from being confused with something very special to you.

Jane Draculette

This little vampire may have the face of an angel, but watch out if she tries to give you a kiss on the cheek—she just might bite your neck!

Habitat
The school yard

What to Do
Tell her that you're already taken, and don't let her get any closer.

Jickup

A tiny monster that you swallow without even knowing it. She's awful. She jumps up and down in your throat and gives you the hiccups.

Habitat
She is invisible and floats around in the air.

What to Do
Hold your nose, and drink a big glass of water to flush her out.

Kaanine

A hideous, insatiable, three-headed monster that drools, barks, and jumps at you, making it impossible to get past him.

Habitat
Walking down the street and at mean people's houses.

What to Do
Throw three balls in different directions to distract each head.

Kalamiteeth

He sniggers as he makes holes in your teeth.

🏠 Habitat
Your mouth, where he settles in with a big appetite.

⚡ What to Do
Bring him to his sworn enemy, the dentist, who will annihilate him with a disgusting paste.

Lunatoad

If you hear strange noises in the middle of the night, it's the Lunatoad! Croaking, hissing, cackling, and making other scary noises—he can make a huge range of sounds.

Habitat
His natural habitat is the garden, but he is also known to roam around the house.

What to Do
Stay calm and let him talk to the moon. He won't hurt you.

Munch-O-Mat

This ogre swallows up your favorite blanket and T-shirts. He usually spits them back out but sometimes shrinks them or changes their color.

🏠 Habitat
He lives in the bathroom, kitchen, or laundry room, where he pretends to be useful.

⚡ What to Do
Don't leave your blanket or clothes lying around.

Mildew Mike

This green terror ruins
everything he touches.

Habitat
He settles into confined humid areas with the hopes of invading the whole house

What to Do
Ask your parents to help you attack him with a sponge and a good household
cleaning product.

Minimaximonster

This horrible little monster has not finished growing. He's the size of an ant right now, but he'll keep growing and growing and growing... How big will he get?

Habitat
Grass

What to Do
Best to mash him with a fly swatter before he gets too big. Otherwise you might run into him later ...

Nannymummy

Just when you least expect her, she appears, motionless and angry.
Without saying a word, she stares you down and stops you in your tracks.

⌂ Habitat
This species is nearly extinct. There are only a few specimens left in museums that go on scaring sprees when they get bored.

◐ Weakness
She is nothing but a rigid mess of skin and bones—no muscles to move, no brain to think.

⚡ What to Do
Unwrap the bandages. Reduced to a skeleton, Nannymummy will be so embarrassed that she'll never come out again.

Nocklessmonster

When you go for a swim, he dunks you or grabs you
by the ankle to pull you under.

Habitat
Lurks around the bottoms of pools

Strength
Shape-shifting, creating creepy shadows and scary reflections.
You can never be sure what he'll look like next.

What to Do
Blow bubbles underwater. Any contact with air
will kill off the Nocklessmonster immediately.

Obsess-O-Tron

When you're just about to finish playing with him, this monster flashes lights, sounds alarms, and generally goes berserk! When your parents call you for dinner, he holds you hostage.

🏠 Habitat
Your home

❗ Strength
You can't stop playing, and he takes advantage of this.
He wants you to never quit.

⚡ What to Do
Shut him down every once in a while.

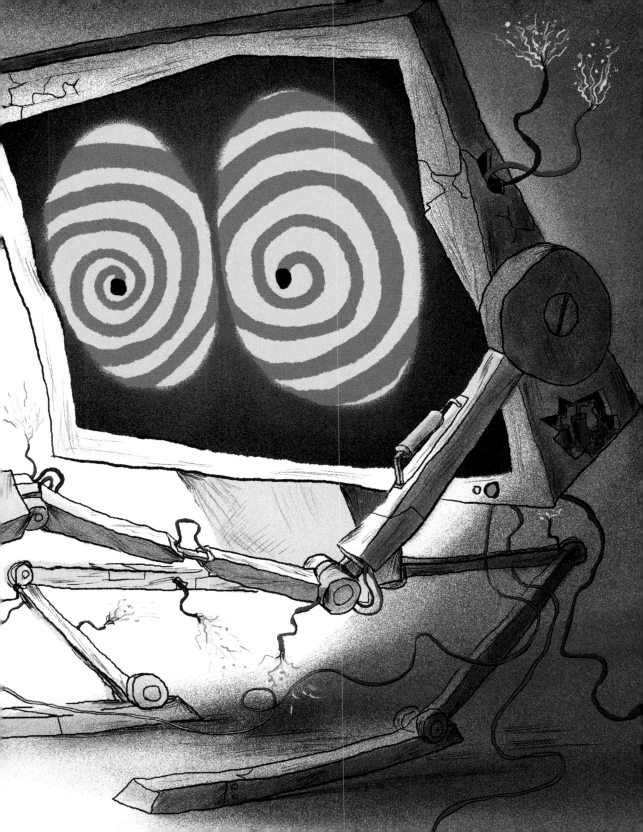

'Orrific

He waits until dark to gobble up anything within reach. Better stay under your blanket and don't leave your hands or feet dangling over the sides.

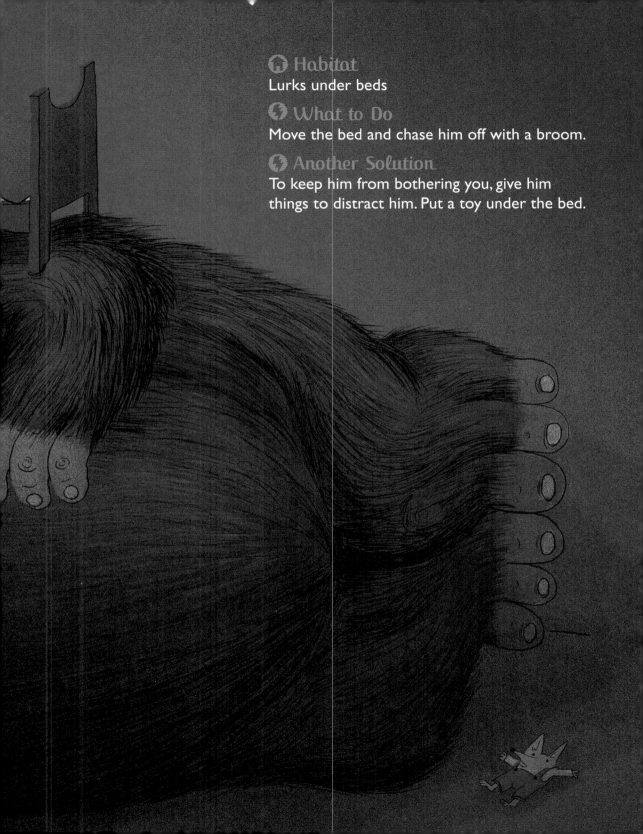

Habitat
Lurks under beds

What to Do
Move the bed and chase him off with a broom.

Another Solution
To keep him from bothering you, give him things to distract him. Put a toy under the bed.

Oversyzload

This big brute makes himself at home in your backpack.
No wonder your shoulders hurt!

⌂ Habitat
Backpacks and book bags

⚡ What to Do
Use a wheeled backpack. The clickety-clackety noise will chase off your stowaway.

Peeyuee

When you least expect it, he sounds the trumpet and releases a nefarious gas to try to poison you.

Habitat
Your underwear

Strength
His surprise attack is worse when it comes from someone standing next to you.

What to do
Hold your nose or wear a gas mask.

Populice

He jumps onto your head and makes himself right at home.
He intends to stay and raise a large family—a very large family

Habitat
Your buddy's hair,
and then yours

What to Do
Exterminate him with
anti-lice shampoo!

Qwiktostick

This monster hangs around you and your friends and won't go away. He is especially prone to clinging to you when you're playing a game, telling a secret, or wanting to be alone with your crush.

Habitat
Playgrounds

Weakness
He hates to be alone.

What to Do
Send him off to cling to a teacher.

Rollinbollin

This sneaky little monster rolls himself up into a ball and throws himself at your legs so you fall down.

Habitat
Strolls innocently around playing fields, parks, or playgrounds.

What to Do
Give him a strong kick to send him as far away as possible.

Snotz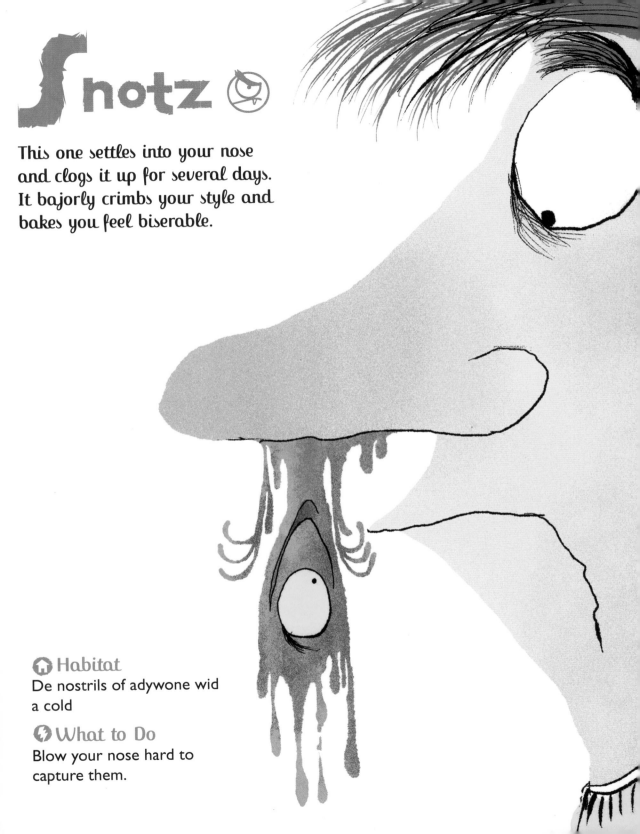

This one settles into your nose and clogs it up for several days. It bajorly crimbs your style and bakes you feel biserable.

Habitat
De nostrils of adywone wid a cold

What to Do
Blow your nose hard to capture them.

Splatterdirter

This creature loves to get your clothes dirty so you get in trouble.

⌂ Habitat
Wherever you like to have fun

⚡ What to Do
Splatterdirter will have nothing to target if you play in a bathing suit!

◑ Weakness: Kind of dumb

Squeakleton

Appears from time to time when your teacher writes on the board. Squeaks, screeches, and generally bothers you.

Habitat
Chalkboards

What to Do
Discreetly flick your previously captured Snotz in his direction.

Temperteaser

A little devil that incites tremendous temper tantrums by poking you with his pitchfork and making you yell at everybody.

Habitat
Can be found anywhere but most often appears at home or in stores

Weakness
His effects don't last long, and when they're over you'll wonder what happened.

What to Do
Find him as quickly as possible, confiscate his pitchfork, and send him packing.

Ultimidator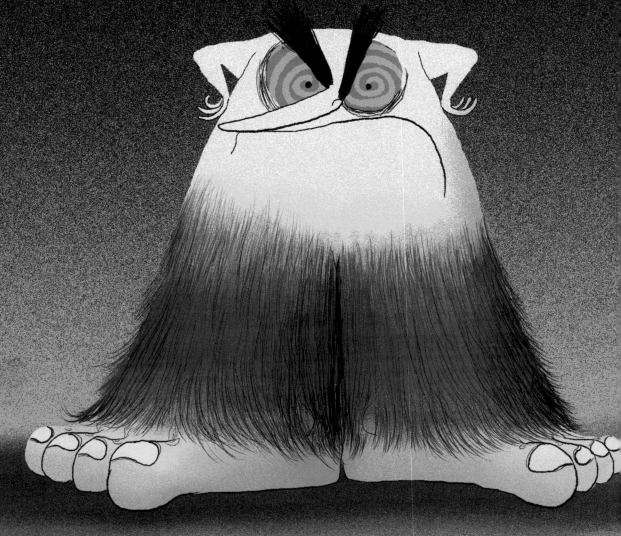

When you want to say something, he stares you down, which makes you blush and renders you speechless—very intimidating!

🏠 Habitat
Mostly at school, where he will sometimes take the form of a teacher

⚡ What to Do
Talk nonsense! He won't expect that, so it'll confuse him.

U*seeum*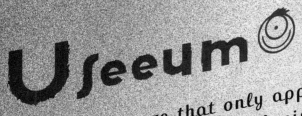

A little creature that only appears for a second! Blink and you'll miss him!

Habitat
Wherever you're bored

Weakness
He's easily frightened.

What to Do
Give him a friendly wave so that he knows you're not a monster.

Vampteether

He tries to bite you even though he doesn't have any teeth yet. His fangs, which are still growing in, make him scream so loudly that he shatters your eardrums.

🏠 Habitat
Home and day care

⚙ What to Do
Give him some vomit porridge to calm him down.

Wheeliebed

He moves your bed around at night, so you
wake up to find your feet on the pillow.
He can even make you fall out of bed.

⌂ Habitat
The bedroom

⚡ What to Do
Add a seatbelt. Whistle really loudly so
that Wheeliebed understands that you are
approaching the station and the end of the line.

X xL

The biggest monster ever.
He wants to take over the world.

⌂ Habitat
Wherever he wants.

❗ Strength
He doesn't even fit on this page.

⚡ What to Do
If you tickle his heel with a
feather, he loses all his strength.

For my little monsters:
Clémence and Louane.
C. L.

For Benjamin L.
R. G.

INSIGHT KIDS

PO Box 3088
San Rafael, CA 94912
www.insighteditions.com

Find us on Facebook: www.facebook.com/InsightEditions
Follow us on Twitter: @insighteditions

First published in English in the United States in 2016 by
Insight Editions, San Rafael, California.

Originally published in France in 2013 by Éditions Glénat as
Mon gros dico de monstres
by C. Leblanc & R. Garrigue.
© 2013 Éditions Glénat
Translation © 2016 by Insight Editions.

Translated from French by Ivanka Hahnenberger and Marc Vilain.

Library of Congress Cataloging-in-Publication Data available.

ISBN: 978-1-60887-709-6

ROOTS of PEACE   REPLANTED PAPER

Insight Editions, in association with Roots of Peace, will plant two trees
for each tree used in the manufacturing of this book. Roots of Peace is
an internationally renowned humanitarian organization dedicated to
eradicating land mines worldwide and converting war-torn lands into
productive farms and wildlife habitats. Roots of Peace will plant two million
fruit and nut trees in Afghanistan and provide farmers there with the skills
and support necessary for sustainable land use.

Manufactured in China by Insight Editions

10 9 8 7 6 5 4 3 2 1

Nannymummy
(Mean)

Nocklessmonstr
(Extremely mean)

Obsess-O-Tron
(Nice)

'Orrific
(Extremely mean)

Oversyzload
(Mean)

Peeyuee
(Nice)

Populice
(Mean)

Qwiktostick
(Nice)

Rollinbollin
(Mean)

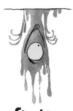
Snotz
(Mean)

Splatterdirter
(Mean)

Squeakleton
(Mean)

Temperteaser
(Mean)

Ultimidator
(Extremely mean)

Useeum
(Nice)

Vampteether
(Nice)

Wheeliebed
(Mean)

XXL
(Mean)

Yasulkinagin
(Nice)

Younosmelloroses
(Nice)

Zalithper
(Nice)

Zebuttbug
(Mean)

Zombizar
(Extremely mean)

Zzeworriez
(Nice)

Alphabeast
(Nice)

Aysnortuptoys
(Mean)

Botherinbobby
(Nice)

Ball-O-Spit
(Mean)

Cravels
(Nice)

Creepinpoop
(Mean)

Danitemare
(Extremely mean)

Drainbane
(Extremely mean)

Embarrassassin
(Nice)

Fogdibrair
(Mean)

Frreezinkold
(Mean)

Fynderzkeeperz
(Nice)

Gickiegoober
(Mean)

Gititoffme
(Nice)

Hallucinato
(Extremely Mea

Horrorkane
(Mean)

Icky Yicky
(Mean)

Jane Draculette
(Nice)

Jickup
(Nice)

Kaaanine
(Extremely Mean)

Kalamiteeth
(Extremely Mean)

Lunatoad
(Nice)

Munch-O-mat
(Extremely Mean)

Mildew Mike
(Mean)

Minimaximon
(Mean)

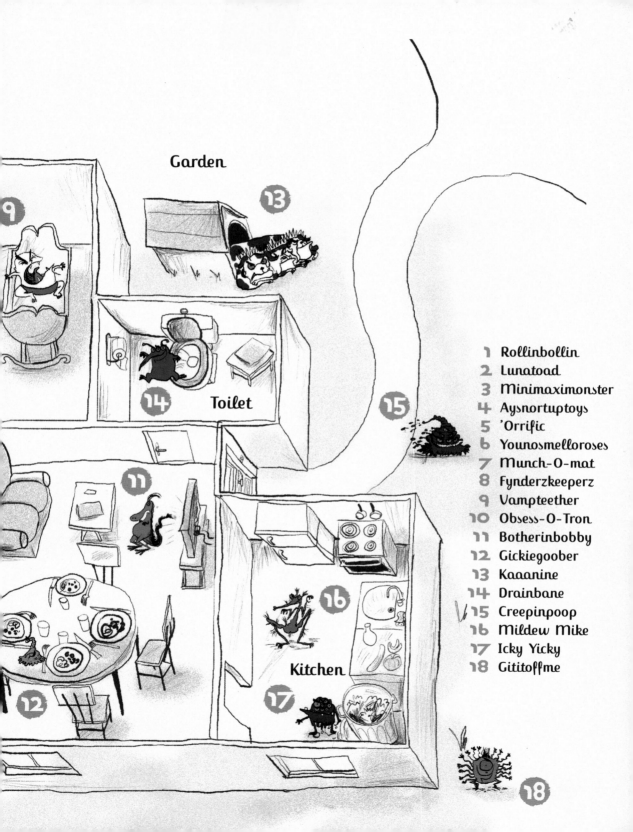

Garden

Toilet

Kitchen

1 Rollinbollin
2 Lunatoad
3 Minimaximonster
4 Aysnortuptoys
5 'Orrific
6 Younosmelloroses
7 Munch-O-mat
8 Fynderzkeeperz
9 Vampteether
10 Obsess-O-Tron
11 Botherinbobby
12 Gickiegoober
13 Kaaanine
14 Drainbane
15 Creepinpoop
16 Mildew Mike
17 Icky Yicky
18 Gititoffme

In the diagram of this house, you'll find some of the monsters listed in this **Monsterpedia** in their natural habitats.

Recipe for Monster Repellent

1 spoonful of spinach, 1 spoonful of broccoli, 1 green bean, 1 brussel sprout, 1 stinging nettle leaf, and 1 cup of soup. Just one sip is enough to ward off even the scariest monster!

Monster Mask

Using paper and colored pens, make the scariest, most terrifying monster mask. Then monsters will want to kiss you instead of eat you.

Monster Trap

Monsters, like children, love candy. Use it to lure them into your trap. Then you can take them to the zoo or turn them into pets.

Tips & Tricks for
Mashing Monsters

Mirror

Monsters don't like looking in mirrors.

Mini-Fortress

To protect yourself from monsters, build a fort using whatever you can find in your home.

Recipe for the Mega Monster-Mashing Magic Potion

10 chocolate bars, 1 mashed banana, 5 of your favorite candies, 1 glass of soda, and a single tiger hair. You'll become 10,000 times more powerful!

and let's not forget

Zzeworries...

They appear when least expected. On their own, Zzeworries are not so hard to chase away, but when they come one after another or in groups, they are more difficult to deal with. Zzeworries can bother and befuddle you, but fortunately they always go away in the end.

Zombizar

This monster is very frightening and strange.
He looks and walks like a zombie.

Habitat
He emerges from the cemetery and heads straight for
you. . . . Maybe he wants to turn you into a zombie!

Weakness: Walks slowly

What to Do
The best trick to try—if you're really clever—is to dig
in his path the biggest hole ever.

Zebuttbug

When you're in class, this little monster makes it impossible to sit still. The sensation can last for a while and force you to keep moving. Some can get really itchy.

🏠 Habitat
Chairs

⚡ What to Do
Stand up on your chair. This will not make Zebuttbug happy.
Turn your math class into a game of Hot Lava.
If she won't go away, a spoonful of pureed prunes should do the trick.

Zalisper

Her curlth tickle your tongue tho itth hard to thpeak.

🏠 Habitat
On your tongue, which she thinkth is a sofa.

⚡ What to Do
Be patient because she is difficult to get rid of. Articulate clearly—that'll shake her up. Don't get upset: Zalisper can be annoying, but she won't affect how you eat or play.

Younosmelloroses

She thinks she's beautiful and swishes around trying to impress you, but she actually smells awful.

🏠 Habitat
She lives in sinks and drains but has been sighted in the schoolyard.

⚡ What to Do
Hold your nose.
Try to make it clear that her sewer smell isn't so great.

Yasulkinagin

He refuses to smile. He sulks.
He wants to spread his bad mood.

🏠 **Habitat**
In places of interest and during dumb activities

⚡ **What to Do**
Cheer him up by reading to him.